For Maple – sweet, talkative
and the best studio companion.

First published 2019 by Macmillan Children's Books
an imprint of Pan Macmillan, 20 New Wharf Road, London N1 9RR
Associated companies throughout the world
www.panmacmillan.com

ISBN: 978-1-5098-6660-1

Text and illustrations copyright © Jessica Meserve 2019

The right of Jessica Meserve to be identified as the author and illustrator of this work
has been asserted by her in accordance with the Copyright, Designs and Patents Act 1988.

135798642

A CIP catalogue record for this book is available
from the British Library.

Printed in China.

# JESSICA MESERVE

# What Clara Saw

(and what the animals did!)

MACMILLAN CHILDREN'S BOOKS

The children of Class B, Dearest Darlings
Primary School, arrived at the wildlife park
with their new teacher, Mr Biggity.
Clara was particularly excited to meet
the animals, especially the tortoise.
She was Clara's favourite.

CHICKENS

SHOP.

LOOS.

EXIT.

FARM

ELEPHANT

TORTOISE

PENGUIN

GIRAFFE

HIPPO

PARROTS

Mr Biggity wanted to see the animals
too, but for an entirely different reason.

"Today, children, I will show you
why humans are better and
more important than
any other animal."

Mr Biggity liked to ask questions he already knew the answer to.

"Can a baboon launch a rocket to the moon?

Can a tortoise write a book, or a giraffe
farm fields for food?

No, no and NO, they can't!

But a human CAN!" said Mr Biggity.
"Humans really are the most marvellous,
the most splendid. Quite the best!"

Clara wasn't so sure.

A sign caught her eye and she stopped to read it.

GOODBYE, ELSIE!

TODAY WE SAY A SAD GOODBYE TO ELSIE, OUR GIANT TORTOISE, AS SHE HEADS TO A NEW HOME FOR ELDERLY ANIMALS.

ELSIE IS 150 YEARS OLD.

"Poor Elsie," said Clara, but nobody was listening . . .
least of all Mr Biggity.

"Hmmm ... interesting, very interesting," said Mr Biggity. "Just as I suspected, this tortoise's head is the size of a tiny walnut. You can't do proper thinking with a brain that size."

But Clara wasn't so sure.

"Do animals feel sad?" she asked.

"Sad? Ha!"
replied Mr Biggity.
"Does a hippo cry?
Does a tortoise
feel teary?

Do penguins whimper with worry?"
(He also liked to answer questions
with more questions!)

"No, no and NO, they don't!
Their brains are far too small for feelings."

But Clara really wasn't sure.

"Can animals talk to each other?"
asked Clara.

"Talk? Ha!
Can a chimp chat?
Can a lemur speak Latin?
Can a parrot put on a play?
Ridiculous!" scoffed Mr Biggity.

"But do they ever help each other?" asked Clara.

"Of course not," he replied. "Grunt, squawk,
hoot and screech, that's all animals do!
They really are such silly and selfish creatures."

Clara still wasn't sure.

She decided to say nothing.

But she saw
*everything.*

She saw the giraffe
and the ostrich . . .

and the elephant too.

"Look at this big beast destroying his tree,"
said Mr Biggity. "Animals just don't care about their things!"

"Can elephants use tools?" wondered one boy.

"Use tools? Ha!" replied Mr Biggity.
"Can an elephant build a house?
Can a rabbit fix a car, or a
squirrel sew a suit?"

"No, no and NO they can't! In fact, animals
don't care about the world around them."

DO NOT
CLIMB
THE
FENCE

Now Clara was absolutely sure that
Mr Biggity knew nothing at all!

"Gather round, Class B. Let's go over
what we have learned today," said Mr Biggity.
"One - animals don't have feelings.
Two - animals can't talk.
Three - animals don't help each other.
Four - animals can't use tools.
And five - animals don't care
about their things."

But nobody was listening, least of all Clara.

"Surely animals do feel love?" whispered the children.

This time Clara asked some questions she already knew the answer to.

"Do animals make friends?

Do animals care for their babies?

Do animals need kindness?"

"Yes, yes and YES,  they do!"
cried all the children.

"Well," interrupted Mr Biggity.
"I know one thing for sure . . .

hippos definitely DON'T have any manners!"

Clara knew something for sure too . . .

All animals really are marvellous
and splendid and quite the best!

And now she had TWO favourites.